The Berenstain Bears

HUG and MAKE UP

When bears are angry
and don't get along,
a hug makes up
for what went wrong.

The Berenstain Bears

HUG and MAKE UP

Stan & Jan Berenstain
with Mike Berenstain

HarperFestival®

A Division of HarperCollins*Publishers*

The Berenstain Bears Hug and Make Up
Copyright © 2006 by Berenstain Bears, Inc.
HarperCollins®, 🐻®, and HarperFestival® are trademarks of HarperCollins Publishers.
All rights reserved. Manufactured in China. No part of this book may be used or reproduced in any manner
whatsoever without written permission except in the case of brief quotations embodied in critical
articles and reviews. For information address HarperCollins Children's Books, a division of
HarperCollins Publishers, 1350 Avenue of the Americas, New York, NY 10019.
Library of Congress catalog card number: 2006925300
ISBN-10: 0-06-057401-1 (trade bdg.) — ISBN-13: 978-0-06-057401-7 (trade bdg.)
ISBN-10: 0-06-057385-6 (pbk.) — ISBN-13: 978-0-06-057385-0 (pbk.)
www.harpercollinschildrens.com
❖
First Edition

Nobody gets along nicely all the time—not the birds in the trees, not the squirrels in their hidey-holes, not the deer in the forest.

Not even the members of the Bear family, who live in the big tree house down a sunny dirt road deep in Bear Country.

Mama Bear, Papa Bear, Brother Bear, Sister Bear, and Honey Bear got along nicely most of the time. They remembered to say "please," "thank you," and "excuse me" most of the time. (Except for baby Honey, who was just learning to talk.)

They were considerate of each other's feelings most of the time. And Brother and Sister tried not to take too long on the phone.

But even happy families like the Bear family, who love each other very much, don't get along all the time. It didn't happen very often, but there were days when the whole family woke up grouchy and got up on the wrong side of the bed.

When it happened, though, it made for a bad day in the tree house.

It could start with Brother or Sister taking too long in the bathroom on a busy school morning. It could start with somebody leaving the cap off the toothpaste tube.

The sign on the door reads:

OCCUPIED
S.B.

It could start with somebody accidentally stubbing a toe. Yes, even Mama sometimes started off on the wrong foot. It didn't help when baby Honey decided to join in and started crying at the top of her lungs.

Things got even worse at breakfast. Manners were forgotten. Nobody said "please pass the jam" or "may I have the honey." The Bears just reached and grabbed. Their dog, Little Lady, got a little worried and hid under the stairs. Goldie, the goldfish, hid in her underwater castle.

Brother finished first and shouted at Sister, who was having a second helping of cereal, "Come on, you slowpoke, or you'll make us late for the school bus!"

"Who are you calling a slowpoke, you dumbhead?" Sister shouted back. "You were the one who made us late yesterday when you forgot to have Mama sign your test paper!"

"That'll be quite enough shouting and name-calling!" roared Papa, banging the table so hard the whole tree house shook.

"And quite enough table banging!" said Mama. "You're worse than the cubs!"

"Grrr!" said Papa, jamming his hat on his head and storming out the door.

Brother and Sister usually sat next to each other on the school bus. But this morning they came onto the bus looking like storm clouds.

"I saved your seats for you," said their friend Lizzy Bruin.

"I wouldn't sit next to him if he were the last bear on earth!" said Sister.

"That goes double for me!" said Brother, stomping to the rear of the bus.

And all through recess and lunch break they refused to have anything to do with each other.

As soon as they got home from school the shouting and arguing started all over again. They argued about where to have their after-school milk and cookies: on the kitchen table or in front of the television.

They argued about which video to watch: *The Bear Stooges* or *The Bearbie Show*. Soon they were rolling around on the floor fighting over the remote.

"I've had quite enough of this fussing and feuding! There'll be no television today!" said Mama. She not only took away the remote, she pulled the plug on the television. "Just sit yourselves down and do your homework, and I don't want to hear another peep out of either of you!"

Brother and Sister sat at the dining-room table and tried to do their homework. But they were so busy looking daggers at each other that they couldn't concentrate.

By the time Papa came in from his shop, the Bears' bad day had become a full-fledged family feud. Little Lady was still hiding under the stairs, and Goldie was still hiding in her castle. Angry silence filled the air.

Grim-faced Brother was trying to reach the next level on one of his video games, but he kept falling short. Tight-lipped Sister was coloring in a coloring book, but she wasn't staying in the lines very well.

Angry Mama was trying to read a magazine.

So Papa sat down glowering and pretended to read the newspaper.

But it's hard for folks who love each other to stay angry all day, especially if they really don't have anything to be angry about.

Sister was the first to break the silence.

"Mama," she said.

"Yes?" said Mama.

"That magazine you're reading," said Sister, starting to giggle. "You've got it upside down!"

"Why, so I do," said Mama with a small giggle of her own.

Now it happens that giggling is as contagious as the twenty-four-hour virus.

More quickly than it takes to tell, the whole Bear family was laughing uproariously. (Except for baby Honey, who until that moment was having a long, quiet nap.)

They were laughing so hard their sides hurt.

They laughed so hard tears rolled down
their cheeks.

And what were they laughing at?
They were laughing at themselves
for wasting a whole day being
angry about nothing.

Little Lady came out from under the stairs,
Goldie came out of her underwater castle,
and Honey Bear saw her once angry family
dry their tears and hug and make up.